MY FIRST
BOOK OF
FAIRY
TALES

MY FIRST
BOOK OF
FAIRY
TALES

Illustrated by Margaret Tarrant

IDEALS CHILDREN'S BOOKS
Nashville, Tennessee

CONTENTS

LITTLE RED RIDING HOOD

One day, Little Red Riding Hood set out through the forest to visit her grandmother, who was ill. On the way, she met a large wolf.

Now the wolf was hungry, but he couldn't eat the girl because there were woodcutters nearby. So he asked her where she was going.

Little Red Riding Hood explained about her grandmother and told the wolf where the old lady lived.

The cunning wolf ran off to grandmother's cottage and gobbled up the old lady in a flash. Then he put on her nightdress and cap and jumped into bed, waiting for Little Red Riding Hood.

At last, she knocked on the door and the wolf said: "Come in."

"Goodness Granny," said Little Red Riding Hood as she went inside, "you must be ill,

your voice sounds so strange."

She went across to the bed to kiss her grandmother.

"Goodness Granny, what rough hairy arms you have!"

"All the better to hug you with, my dear," said the wolf.

"Goodness Granny, what big ears you have!"

"All the better to hear you with, my dear," replied the wolf.

"Goodness Granny, what huge teeth you have!"

"All the better to gobble you up with!" snarled the wolf springing out of bed.

Little Red Riding Hood ran for her life. One of the woodcutters heard her screams and rushed to her rescue. Down came his axe on the hairy head and the wolf lay dead on the ground. Little Red Riding Hood was saved, but you can be sure that she never talked to strangers again.

CINDERELLA

Once upon a time, there lived a girl called Cinderella, whose life was made wretched by her stepsisters. They made her into their servant; she had to cook and clean, wash and iron and wait on them hand and foot. In return, they pinched and slapped her and were never pleased with anything she did.

One day, a royal invitation arrived asking the sisters to the King's ball. There was great excitement: the house bustled all day long with dressmakers, jewellers, hairdressers, and dancing masters.

At last, the sisters were ready and swept off without even thanking Cinderella for all her hard work.

Cinderella sank exhausted onto her stool by the fire. "I wish I could go to the ball," she said and a tear slipped down her face.

"You shall go to the ball!" exclaimed a voice.

Cinderella looked up and saw a little old lady.

"I am your Fairy Godmother, do as I say quickly and your wish will come true."

Cinderella did as she was told. She fetched a pumpkin from the garden, mice from the cellar and lizards from the flowerpots.

Her Fairy Godmother waved her magic wand and they turned into a golden coach with six horses and footmen.

Cinderella's ragged dress became a ball-gown embroidered with jewels and her bare feet were in glass slippers that shone like diamonds.

"Go," said the Godmother, "but leave before the clock strikes midnight or the spell will end."

Cinderella was the success of the ball. The Prince fell in love with the beautiful and

mysterious young woman. Cinderella forgot the time, midnight struck and she tore herself from the Prince's arms. As she ran home, she lost a glass slipper on the palace stairs.

The Prince found the slipper, but not Cinderella. He travelled the Kingdom searching for his lost love. He tried the glass slipper on the foot of every woman, including Cinderella's cruel sisters, but it fitted no one.

In despair, he cried: "Is there no one else here?"

"There's me," said Cinderella. Her sisters pushed her away, but the Prince asked Cinderella to try on the slipper. It fitted perfectly. Cinderella married the Prince and they lived happily ever after.

THE UGLY DUCKLING

Once upon a time, a duck hatched six of the prettiest yellow, fluffy ducklings ever seen. But the seventh duckling, which hatched from a huge egg, was the ugliest duckling on the farm. It was big and grey and from the start everyone disliked it.

His own brothers and sisters kept saying: "If only the cat would get you, you hideous object!"

His own mother wished him far away and the hens pecked him.

He was so unhappy that he ran away. As he flew, he scared the little birds in the bushes. "It's because I'm so ugly," sighed the duckling and a tear rolled down his beak. He met the wild ducks.

"Gosh," they quacked, "you're ugly." Everywhere he went it was the same and

the ugly duckling became more and more miserable.

Winter came, it was bitterly cold. The duckling had to keep swimming to prevent his pond from freezing altogether. At last he grew faint, lay quite still and froze fast in the ice.

Early in the morning, a farmer found him. He broke the ice and took him home to the warm farmhouse kitchen where the duckling revived.

The children wanted to play with the duckling, but he thought they meant to hurt him so he flew around the room. He crashed into the milk can, upset the butter and knocked the flour to the floor. The farmer's wife chased him. Luckily the door was open and he escaped.

When spring arrived, the ugly duckling could not face life any more. One day, he saw three beautiful swans on a lake.

"I will fly towards the royal birds and they

will peck me to death because I am so ugly."

So he flew out on to the water until the swans saw him and rushed towards him. He closed his eyes and waited for death.

Instead, the swans swam round him making friendly noises. The duckling asked them why.

"You are one of us," they replied. "Look at yourself."

So he opened his eyes and saw his reflection in the water. A magnificent white swan looked back at him. He was no longer the ugly duckling and all the other swans bowed to him.

BEAUTY AND THE BEAST

Once upon a time, there lived a girl who was as beautiful as she was good. Her father called her Beauty and he loved her very much. One day he had to go on a long journey, but he promised to bring Beauty back a rose.

The merchant travelled all day and by nightfall he was quite lost. Stumbling through a wood, he went down an overgrown path. At the end he found a castle; the door was open so the merchant went inside where a servant gave him food and a soft bed for the night.

In the morning, the merchant looked for the master of the house to thank him. He entered a glorious rose garden and picked a rose for Beauty. As he cut the stem, there was a great roar. Terrified, the merchant fell to the ground.

A huge, hairy hand pulled him to his feet; a creature with the head of a monster and the shape of a human roared at him:

"Ungrateful man, why have you stolen my rose?"

The shaking merchant explained the gift for his daughter.

"I kill anyone who steals my roses," said the Beast, "but if you bring me your daughter, I will not kill you. Promise or die."

The merchant promised and went home.

Three months later, he returned and gave Beauty to the Beast. Beauty did her best to hide her fear, but the Beast was more hideous than she had imagined.

In spite of his looks, the Beast was kind to Beauty. One evening, watching her quietly, he said to her:

"Beauty, will you marry me?"

"No Beast," replied Beauty. The Beast gave a great sigh and his face crumpled with

sadness. After that he asked Beauty the question every night and her answer was always the same.

Although life with the Beast was not terrible, Beauty was homesick; she longed to see her father. She began to look miserable and ill and the Beast, afraid that she would die, agreed to let her go home for a month if she promised to return.

Beauty promised and went home to her father, who was overjoyed to see her.

Beauty forgot time. Two months passed, then she dreamed about the Beast. He was thin and mournful and looked as if he was about to die. Beauty was filled with remorse at breaking her promise and rushed back to the castle. She found Beast lying in the rose garden.

"Beast!" she cried, "Please do not die, I will marry you twenty times if only you will not die." She flung her arms around his neck

and kissed him.

At that instant the garden was filled with light and music. Beauty looked at the Beast in astonishment: he had changed into a handsome young prince who gazed at her lovingly.

"Thank you Beauty," said the prince. "Your unselfish love has broken the spell of a wicked fairy and I am myself. Now will you marry me?"

I expect you can guess Beauty's answer.

SNOW WHITE

Once upon a time there lived a very vain Queen. She gazed at herself in mirrors all day. One of the mirrors was magical and when the Queen looked in it she said:

"Mirror, mirror on the wall,
Who is the fairest one of all?"

The mirror replied:

"Beautiful Queen, so proud and tall,
You are the fairest one of all."

One day, the Queen asked the mirror her usual question and the mirror replied:

"Beautiful Queen, so proud and tall,
Snow White is the fairest one of all."

The Queen flew into a terrible rage. Princess Snow White was her step-daughter and the Queen was already very jealous of her. She commanded her huntsman to take Snow White into the forest and kill her.

The huntsman obeyed, but when he came to kill Snow White, he pitied her and set her free. So Snow White wandered through the trees and found a little house. She was so tired that, when there was no reply to her knocking, she let herself in and lay down on a little bed and fell asleep.

When she woke she was surrounded by dwarfs! "Who are you?" they asked kindly. Snow White told them her story and they decided that she must stay with them. Snow White happily agreed.

Far away in the palace the Queen asked the mirror who was now the most beautiful. It replied:

"Beautiful Queen, so proud and tall,
You were once the fairest of all,
But Snow White lives with the dwarfs so
small
And she is the fairest one of all."

The Queen was furious that Snow White was still alive, so she disguised herself as a pedlar woman and travelled to the dwarfs' house. When the pedlar woman knocked on the door, Snow White bought some ribbons for her bodice.

"Let me help you lace them properly," said the wicked Queen and she pulled them tighter and tighter until Snow White could not breathe and fell as if dead.

When the dwarfs came home they cut the ribbons and Snow White revived. The dwarfs told Snow White never to let anyone into the house again.

Meanwhile the Queen spoke to her mirror

again, but the mirror said:

"Beautiful Queen, so proud and tall,
Snow White is the fairest one of all."

This time the Queen shook with rage. "Snow White shall die," she cried. She poured poison into one half of a rosy apple. She found Snow White in the garden of the dwarfs' house. "Take this red apple as a present, my dear," said the evil woman.

"Oh I mustn't," said Snow White.

"I will cut it in half and eat it with you," said the wily Queen. So Snow White bit into her half of the apple and fell dead at the Queen's feet.

When the dwarfs found her they tried every remedy, but they could not rouse her. At last, they sorrowfully admitted that she was dead. She looked so beautiful that they made her a glass coffin and wrote in letters of gold on the

lid: "Snow White, a Royal Princess", placing it on a mountain.

A Prince came by and saw the glass coffin. He gazed at the beautiful Princess inside. The dwarfs told the Prince her sad story.

"I cannot live without looking at her," said the Prince. "Please let me take her with me."

At first the dwarfs refused, but in the end they were sorry for the Prince and agreed.

As the Prince's servants raised the coffin, one of them tripped and the jolt shook the piece of poisoned apple from Snow White's throat. She opened her eyes, and, sitting up, saw the Prince.

"I love you more than anything in the world," he said. "Please marry me." So she did. She rode away with her Prince, taking the dwarfs' wedding gift – a beautiful fawn.

When the wicked Queen heard about the wedding of Snow White, she burst her heart with rage and died.

GOLDILOCKS AND THE THREE BEARS

Once upon a time, there were three bears. There was a big bear, a middle-sized bear and a little, baby bear and they lived in a cottage in a wood.

One morning, the three bears made porridge for breakfast. It was too hot to eat, so they left it and went for a walk while it cooled down. A little girl called Goldilocks came wandering along and saw their pretty house.

She peeped in at the window and saw three steaming bowls of porridge.

"Mmmmm, they look good," she said and went inside.

She tried the porridge in the big bowl: it burnt her tongue. Then she tasted the porridge in the middle-sized bowl: it wasn't sweet enough. So she tried the porridge in the little bowl: it was just right, so she ate it all up.

Then she tried all the chairs; but Big Bear's chair was much too large, Middle-Sized Bear's chair was too hard, and Little Bear's chair was too small and she broke it.

By now she was feeling very tired, so she went upstairs and saw three beds. The big bed was too enormous, the middle-sized bed was too hard, and the little bed was just the right size, so she laid down and fell asleep.

The three bears came home to eat their porridge, but when they saw their bowls, Big Bear growled:

"Someone's been eating my porridge."

"Someone's been eating my porridge," said Middle-Sized Bear.

"Someone's been eating my porridge and has eaten it all up," said Little Bear.

They looked around and saw their chairs.

"Someone's been sitting in my chair," said Big Bear.

"Someone's been sitting in my chair," said

Middle-Sized Bear.

"Someone's been sitting in my chair and has broken it," cried Little Bear.

Then they went upstairs. "Someone's been sleeping in my bed," growled Big Bear.

"Someone's been sleeping in my bed," said Middle-Sized Bear.

"Someone's been sleeping in my bed and she's still there," squeaked Little Bear at the top of his voice.

The noise woke Goldilocks, who leapt out of bed in fright at seeing the three bears. She jumped out of the window and ran home as fast as her legs could carry her.

THE PRINCESS AND THE PEA

Once upon a stormy night, a princess knocked at a castle gate. At least, she said she was a princess, but all the Queen could see was a dripping girl with muddy shoes.

"We'll see," thought the Queen: she wanted a real princess to marry her son.

The Queen put a pea on the mattress of the guest bed. Then she piled twenty mattresses on top of the pea. That night the Princess slept on them all.

"How did you sleep?" asked the Queen in the morning.

"Very badly," said the Princess. "There was something hard under the mattresses. I tossed and turned all night and I'm black and blue this morning."

The Prince married her, for only a real Princess could have such delicate feeling.

JACK AND THE BEANSTALK

Once upon a time, a poor widow sent her son Jack to sell their only cow. On the way to market Jack met a butcher who gave him a bag of beans for the cow. Jack's mother was so angry with Jack when he arrived home that she threw the beans out of the window.

The next day, a huge beanstalk had grown beside the cottage. It was so big that the top disappeared into the clouds. It was too tempting for Jack, who climbed up it. When he got to the top he met a fairy.

"You must be Jack," said the fairy. "I know all about you." She told Jack how, many years before, his father had been killed by a giant who had taken all the family's riches.

Jack was determined to find the giant and punish him for his wickedness, so he set out

47

for the ogre's castle.

When he got there he slipped inside and hid. Soon the giant arrived home and in a voice of thunder called:

"Fee fi fo fum,
I smell the blood of an Englishman."

But although he searched everywhere he could not find Jack, so he shouted for his hen.

"Lay," roared the giant, and the hen laid a huge golden egg. She continued to lay, but the giant, tired after hunting all day, fell asleep.

Jack crept out of his hiding place and, snatching up the hen, ran to the top of the beanstalk and slithered down to his mother.

The hen laid many golden eggs for Jack, and soon he and his mother were rich. But Jack could not forget that the giant had killed his father and was determined to take his

revenge. So, once more, he climbed the beanstalk and hid in the giant's castle.

When the giant came home he roared,

"Fee fi fo fum,
I CAN smell the blood of an Englishman.
When I catch you I'll eat you alive."

Jack jumped out of his hiding place and ran like mad for the beanstalk. The giant began to scramble down after him, but Jack landed first and, grabbing an axe, hacked at the beanstalk until it crashed to the ground, killing the giant instantly. Jack, his mother, and the hen lived happily together.

PUSS IN BOOTS

Once upon a time, a miller died and left nothing to his youngest son but a cat. The young man was miserable.

"I might as well skin you for a pair of gloves," he said to the cat. "You'd be more use to me dead than alive."

"Now that's just where you're wrong," said the cat. "I'd be more use to you alive than dead."

The young man was speechless with astonishment: the cat could talk.

The cat continued, "Dear master, give me a pair of leather boots and I will make you rich."

So the young man gave the cat a fine, little pair of leather boots and Puss set off to make his master's fortune.

First, Puss caught two big rabbits and

M.W.Tarrant

presented them to the King.

"A present for you, Sire, with the compliments of my master, the Marquis of Carabas."

The king was amused by the talking cat and thanked him.

When Puss heard that the King was out driving with his beautiful daughter, he bounded across the fields to the castle of an ogre telling his master to follow.

Puss rang the doorbell and, when the ogre answered, he bowed low and said that he had heard the ogre was a clever magician able to change himself into different animals.

The ogre was very vain and invited the cat into the castle to see his magic. He muttered a spell and became a huge lion.

Puss arched his back and bushed his tail but congratulated the ogre on his cleverness.

"Now how about a very small creature, such as a mouse?" suggested the cunning cat.

In a twinkling, the ogre became a tiny squeaking mouse and Puss gobbled him up.

When his master arrived, Puss dressed him in the ogre's fine clothes and together they waited for the King's coach. As it drove up, they bowed low.

The King said to his daughter, "Why, it's the talking cat I told you about, my dear."

"And this," said Puss, "is my master the Marquis of Carabas and his castle. We have prepared a feast for you."

After that, the Princess and the Marquis fell in love and were married. Puss was given a new pair of boots and led the wedding procession.

THE SLEEPING BEAUTY

Once upon a time, a King and Queen had a beautiful baby. All the fairies in the land were invited to the christening of the little Princess. All except one who was wicked.

At the christening, the fairies gave the baby Princess gifts of beauty, kindness, courage, and cleverness.

The ceremony had just finished when the wicked fairy flew in at the door.

"I'll teach you to leave me out," she hissed as she darted towards the cradle. "My gift to you little Princess, is that you will prick your finger on a spindle and die."

She flew away, her shrieks of laughter echoing through the palace.

The King and Queen were terrified, but the good fairies, although unable to stop the spell, promised that the Princess would not

die when she pricked her finger, but would fall asleep for a hundred years.

On her fifteenth birthday, the Princess played hide and seek. Looking for someone, she went into a turret where she had never been and saw an old woman spinning.

"What are you doing?" asked the Princess.

"Spinning, Your Highness," replied the old woman.

"May I try?" said the Princess. The old lady gave her the spindle.

Immediately, the Princess pricked her finger and fell into a deep sleep. The King laid her on her embroidered bed. The spell was very strong and soon the whole palace fell asleep. A thick hedge of thorns grew round and hid it. As years passed, no one could even remember where the palace had been.

One hundred years later, a prince was hunting in the forest when he saw the towers of a palace above the trees. He rode towards

61

them, but his way was barred by a thick thorn hedge. He cut a path through and found a huge doorway. Opening it, he entered the enchanted palace. Ignoring the sleeping figures all around him, he searched every room. Finally, he opened a door and found Sleeping Beauty.

The Prince kissed her and broke the spell. She woke and so did the whole palace. The Prince married the Princess and they lived happily ever after.